BEST KEPT SECRETS OF MORTALITY

Poems by Louis Phillips

For

Pat, Ian & Priyanka

and, of course,

Mateo.

Published by World Audience, Inc.
(www.worldaudience.org)
New York, NY
worldaudience@gmail.com

ISBN 9798873290543

Copyright ©2024, Louis Phillips

The publisher and editor-in-chief of World Audience Publishers is M. Stefan Strozier (www.mstefanstrozier.com).

Copyright notice: All work contained within is the sole copyright of its author, 2024, and may not be reproduced without consent. World Audience (www.worldaudience.org) is a global consortium of artists and writers, producing quality books and magazines.

TABLE OF CONTENTS

The Happiness Machine..7
Pretty Much..8
S.O.S. 9
The Goddess of Days...10
King Kong in Shakespeare's Hamlet..........................11
A Short History of Optics..13
Why Human Beings are not Things............................14
Striptease..15
Wishes..16
All Things Mine...17
Fate...18
Unspeakable...19
Pick Up Lines...20
Love Poem...21
Shore Lines..22
Bees in Ms. Emily's Amherst Garden.........................24
The Well of Memory...25
Sideshow..26
Squawk...27
The Maltese Falcon...28
Blizzard..29
True Confessions Poetry...30
Epic..31
Foreign Language..32
Sifting the Ashes...33
Irises..34
Trying To Fall Asleep...35
Torrents...36

Slice...41
What Do Poets Want?..42
Sending the Old Lady a Packet of Sorrows...............43
All in a Summer's Day...44
Making Love...45
Is It Not Obvious..46
Bystander..47
Ask Alexa..48
Pharma...49
My Life with the Big Cats..50
Nightwalkers...52
The Chart..53
The Incredible Shrinking Poem...............................54
Hauntings...55
50 Degrees of Separation...57
Ambition...58
Bad Ends...59
Fly Ash..60
Carpe Diem...62
A Poem about a Monsoon.......................................63
Sahara...64
Change of Address..65
Out of Touch..66
Wireless...68
How to Ruin a Perfectly Fine Poem.........................69
Mugged...70
About the Author..71
Bibliography...72

THE HAPPINESS MACHINE

Because the Happiness Machine,
Sits on our front porch,
Awaiting to be assembled,
Days appear to be much shorter
Than absolutely necessary.
Too many moving parts,
Batteries not included.
When I finally lifted
The Happiness Machine from its box
To carry it inside,
The instruction sheet
Mysteriously disappeared.

PRETTY MUCH

Often smart people
End up stupid,
Stupid people
End up rich,
While rich people
End up
Much more rich
Than they had been
When they started out,
Whereas the poor –
Well, the poor end up
Pretty much the same
Everywhere.

S.O.S.

It is true.
Your reputation is in danger.

This poem
Has arrived

In the nick of Time
To save you

From any further
Embarrassment:

You can now hold
Your head high,

Because your taste
In reading

Only the best poetry
Is impeccable.

THE GODDESS OF DAYS

The goddess of days is lonely.
Monday has disappeared.
There is nothing I can do
To console her.
All I can say:
Her light leaning on me
Weighs more
Than all the planets put together.

KING KONG IN SHAKESPEARE'S HAMLET

"He took me by the wrist and held me hard,"
    —*Ophelia*

Not quite as large as Denmark,
King Kong strides
Battlement, unfolds himself
To make mince meat

Of Bernardo. Bitter cold,
Sick at heart Kong pries
Elsinore from its foundation,
Swats biplanes out of skies,

Depositing, like No Deposit,
No Return bottles,
Pilots, servants, valiant soldiers,
& ageing ghosts, all souls in transit.

If Hamlet's father lived forever
Wd we give the Prince
A second thought?
From Skull Island, strolling players

Arrive with scripts in hand,
Pledging to please
The royal audience.
Monkeyshines will not ease

The conscience of our Giant Ape
Whose mind is
A banana republic of grievances.
Reynaldo, servant to Polonius

Announces a tax on taxidermy:
(*A huge organ swells*).
Kong, with Ophelia in his paw,
Struggles with soliloquies.

While poor Ophelia
Is harrowed with fear & wonder.
"Thou art a scholar. Speak
To it, Horatio. Look! Her under-

Wear is torn." (This filmed version
Is rated X), Kong,
Stunned by Beauty, climbs
The Empire's highest tower. The virgin

Screams, Biplanes come back.
Fortinbras: "Go, bid the soldiers shoot!"
Kong, bullet-rivened with a broken heart,
Crashes to earth. Fade to black

A SHORT HISTORY OF OPTICS

Impenetrable to the last,
My mind is not as coherent
As I wd like it to be.
Today, for example, I went

To the local library
& checked out
Euclid's *History of Optics,*
Which I guess is about

Seeing: "The straight lines
drawn from the eyes diverges
to embrace the magnitude.'
seen..." Hmm. I soon find

I shd have borrowed a spy thriller.
Returning Euclid,
I could not help but notice
A young redhead clad

In short shorts & a halter
With a come hither attitude.
My eyes diverged straight forth
To embrace her magnitudes.

WHY HUMAN BEINGS ARE NOT THINGS

The sadness of objects
Is not easily explained.

STRIPTEASE

All right, I'm taking everything off:
The whole shebang,
Not one word with any clothing.
Camouflage: the world freaks out
With nakedness,
Until even our flesh falls off,
Skeletons rattling the woods.
Hold your life up
To dazzling sunlight
& see how long a shadow
It casts. Alcohol & drugs
Won't help. Bang!
Poetry, drag your sorry ass over here.
I don't know what I'm doing,
But I'm doing it.

WISHES

Waterwish. Firewish
Rising out of ashes.
Geniis out of bottles
Need not apply. *Be careful,
what you wish for.*

Living with my parents,
My grandmother recited
*If wishes were horses,
Beggars wd ride,*
Causing my 6 yr old mind

To imagine cities of horses
With beggars
On their backs. Today,
I feel sorry for any person
Cursed with 3 wishes.

Does rain wish
To fall upwards?
When I was young
I wished to be older
Today? guess what?
 Mist in the evening.
 Remember what the mother
 Of Harry Crews sd:
 "Wish in one hand
 And shit in the other.

"See which one fills up first."

ALL THINGS MINE

Arms reaching forth
As if the horizon
Were theirs for the taking,
Gestures of small children
Strain to larger worlds,

I see my own mother
Holding me in her arms.
I struggle against
Being held back.
My hands open then grasp
At air, at water,
At all things mine!

How wrong I was.
Now that I am ripe
For the world's taking,
How little of the world is mine.

FATE

The gods hand out
Lottery cards
With all the numbers filled out.

UNSPEAKABLE

4 in the afternoon:
Faint glow
In the gas lamps,
Light as tender
As any desire unspoken.
In the park's fading light.
Children gather
With their toys
& their thoughts.

Into the fog
A skiff upon the Aarstrasse
Disappears. I cd be
on that skiff.
On the verge of disappearing.
I speak in order to discover
What I most want to say
When it is not yet dark.

PICK UP LINES

The woman at the end of the bar
Was humming
"Cat's in the cradle."
When she lifted her head
She spoke to me
In a pure lyrical soprano
Unforgettable poetry:
"If you keep smiling at me
I'll knock your fuckin' teeth
Down your fuckin' throat."

LOVE POEM

The trout, according to Jeffries,
"Looks like a living arrow,
Formed to shoot through the water."

This summer
I have watched grown men
Wade for hours

In hope of achieving one.
Then when the trout
With spots resembling

"Cochineal and gold dust,"
Had been "killed" then
Let go again,

An arrow thru water,
The unhooking of the barb,
This freeing

Into cold &
Swirling mysteries vast,
I thought of my own long marriage,

Inborn with tiny breathings.

SHORE LINES

Mornings.
With their attendant glories,
Come and go
While History happens
In places we did not think to look.

   2.

Seasons
With major & minor joys,
Slip in & out
Of our consciousness,
Wind whoop, raucous jays,
Etc. etc. et. al. ibid
Faint odors of decay
Whirling about,
Late afternoons, early evenings
Stirring with subtleties,
The old Spring tease.

Oceans
With numerous currencies
Lure us with creatures,
Rising & falling,
Luminescence seas
Of dull shine, etc. et.al
Faint odors of decay,
Red skies at night
(Sailors' delight).
No matter how far we sail,

Years before the mast,
We must not fail
To return to shore.

BEES IN MS. EMILY'S AMHERST GARDEN

Bees have no truck
With anything false –
Anything unnatural
Awaiting bedrock

Of another Spring,
Thickening swarm
Of early warmth
Bruised with awakenings,

Rumors of life full round.
Buzz buzz
Of the honeycombed *is* –
From the ground up

I comprehend nothing,
That is unsweetened
By the push & pull
Of a new season swinging into view.

THE WELL OF MEMORY

The deeper I drill,
The colder
The water.

SIDESHOW

"Come. Weep for Adonais. He is dead,"
See him inside the tent. $15.00 a head.

SQUAWK

The old black man with no teeth,
Snow was fast falling
So he swept the cafe's sidewalk,
Shouting at passers-by:
"I don't want no weak woman.
I'm not fucking no weak woman."
He glanced in my direction,
But did not know me.
He looked straight beyond me.
To no one in particular he asked:
"What are you squawking at me for?
I don't understand no squawked."

THE MALTESE FALCON

"I do like a man
who tells me right out
that he's looking out for himself,"

But who is looking out for this poem?
Not readers precisely.
They wish to be moved or entertained

& these words cannot do it
With the same panache as a movie
Crisp with oddball characters,

Many of whom carry revolvers.
As for critics, I say "Give 'em the bird."
All this to say

That many realities are a long way off,
So I have decided
To look out for myself.

This poem, unfortunately,
Completely disarmed,
Has to go it alone.

BLIZZARD

T'ao Ch'ien sd:
"Hunger drove me
Into the world."
Yes. What a lash
Hunger is.
I work hard,
Get little
For my pains.
Yet, falling snow says:
"Pay attention:
I'll show you real work."

TRUE CONFESSIONS POETRY

Every word
In this short poem
Is older than you are.

EPIC

O.K. I left Homer
On the porch.

A family of wrens
Made a nest

On *The Odyssey*.
Just my luck

To be surrounded
By animals

Who cannot read.

FOREIGN LANGUAGES

I am too old to fight crocodiles
With my bare hands.
I'll let Johnny Weissmuller
Do it for me. On television
Black actors in bare feet
Ferociously stomp on sand
Delivered to M-G-M's back lot
(*Thud, thud, thud* subtitles say).
Spear carriers leap up & down:
Gloobo Hut Hit Fooey unjab:
Speaking Esperanto language
Of Hollywood script-writers.
Worshippers of the Leopard God,
Bones through their noses,
Thrust fists into the air,
Shout *gubba gubba dreg upo,*
Sounding exactly like my critics.
When African natives speak
Unbo frete lappo lappo bo Enibi.
Subtitles read:
Speaking a foreign language.
Thank you for telling me.

SIFTING THE ASHES

How shall we ever know
The truth about ourselves?
Time sifts the ashes,
But we shall be long gone.
.
Our friends, God bless them,
Attempt to protect ourselves
From ourselves &
From our enemies,
While our enemies are kind,
Showering us with envy
and/or bitterness.
The natural world,
With its many beasts
& monsters, & billions
Of scattered human beings
Manifest indifference.
Tho sometimes spirits,
Ghosts on stilts,
Memories stained & smudged
Enter our time & space,
Shaking their heads with wonder.

IRISES

What we did, where we were,
Who we were then,

I no longer remember,
& every so often names escape me,

But your face remains firm
Where once my heart beat wildly,

Remembering your wide skirt,
Your laughter

That made days open & close,
So today I bring these words

Opening & closing, closing &
Opening. I bring them to you

Because the flower lady
On our corner

Had sold out the irises
Which you love so much.

TRYING TO FALL ASLEEP

In the City that never sleeps.
I am trying to escape
Counting electric sheep
By shouting at my sons,
Teen-agers, drinking & laughing
Loudly in our living room
At sex jokes & Blade Runners.

I have awakened my wife
From her own sound sleep.
Go back to sleep, I tell her,
But she is not listening to me.
She knows our sons
Will not listen to anything
I might tell them.

1, 2, 3, 4, breathe in, breathe out.

Did I ever listen to my old man?
I want to embrace
My mistress Sleep, flailing against
The matter-of-fact of knowing
What sons must learn the hard way,
How to get on with one's own life

Without hurting too many other people.

TORRENTS

Even as Tuesday,
Certain as Death & Taxes,
Pours down upon me
A Torrent of Fears,
Muddled with lost loves,
Old age hammers
My ear-drums. Memories,
Like unpaid bills,
Refuse to lie down quietly
In Return to Sender box.

Flush with anger,
I Tap the Redo app
One too many times.
Nothing is undone.
I don't know what I'm doing,
But I am doing it
Hiking forward is one thing,
Going back is another.

With a hue & cry
The day undoes its laces
Repeating *kill-death*
Kill-dee, kill-death
Sharper than Longspur,
The meadow beyond
Opens to astonishments
Glimpsed at odd hours,

A rush of creatures,
Short-lived on sure footing,
Deer in small clusters
Breathing the same air I do,
A swell of small miracles
Rushing out-of-control
Through my head:
Who's alive? Who's dead?
Imagination's wild ride,
Bump, skid, slide
One distracted guide
To monuments of loss.

Growing up in Florida,
In the tiniest house
On the block, Hansel
& Gretel nowhere in sight,
Everglades of sawgrass,
Seminoles wrestling
Alligators & racism galore,
Back & forth-ness
Of random, incoherent.
Growing angers, sweep
Of small mercies,
My younger sisters
Playing in the yard,
My mother in a clothing store,
Working, working,
My father in Browning King,
Only 2 blocks away,
Even on days,
When nights before,
His ulcers punched his clock
overtime. A dozen years

I walked those blocks,
Or sat in the movie theater
(Was it The Colony?)
Waiting for my parents
To get off work
To drive me home,
My mind a tempest
Of this & that, that &
This, rapid rewind,
Of news, odd facts, books
Mingled with books,
Borrowed from the library

Where I worked
From Junior High
Thru High School.
Stray kittens at the door.

Backward glances
Arrive in a singular line
I heard in a b&w film
About barnstorming pilots
Who fly upside down
& practice wing-walking,
Then leap into the air,
Parachuting into the ocean.
Those daredevils,
So loosely cavalier,
Made my young self feel
As if I had never lived,
Never risked my neck
On anything dangerous.

In the tumble of dialogue
The lead female sd:
Angels don't wear pants.

SLICE

Each word is a weapon:
Sharpen its edges
Until it slices thru the page
Until it draws blood
From unsuspecting readers.

WHAT DO POETS WANT?

Words that fit
Double-parked
In tight spaces.
Jaunce, for example.

Or moon-simple.
I'll stick them
In lines 4 & 5
& hope

Someone will notice.

SENDING THE OLD LADY A PACKET OF SORROWS

Overnight delivery service
Decided to leave a package
On the old lady's front porch
Where she wd stumble over it
In the morning. I suggested
Using fancy wrapping paper
& tying it with a wide red bow
But co-workers only laughed.
The wireless piped in music:
In your old Kentucky home,
Cry no more, my lady
For me, it took years
At the Sorrow Seed company
To learn what Management
& older workers already knew:
Nobody dies merely once.

ALL IN A SUMMER'S DAY

Dawn, with her rosy-fingers
& exaltation of larks,
Has washed her hands of me,
Wanders off,
Without even a proper farewell.
She cd care less whether
I live or die. So much for morning.

The bandersnatch universe
Sticks its claws into me.
I wish I cd say as optimists do.
That sweet are the uses
Of adversity. All adversity does
Is feed the fires of envy.
In the end, what are we all?
A feast for the gods.
Or, if not a feast, at least

Succulent morsels choked down
Without one serious thought
Behind them. *Tiralira loo.*

MAKING LOVE

What bears this traffic
Is not a road,
But promise,
Numinous giving forth
& giving forth again,
Bone bewilderment,
Hair that bites,
Teeth touching
Enamel to enamel,
Among the hardest substance
Known,
With sleeping hands
Awake,
& tiny moments
That slide
This way & that,
Raindrops
On glass
Bulging.

IS IT NOT OBVIOUS

Sylvia Plath wrote about a mirror:
"I am not cruel, only truthful."
How easy it might be to tell the truth
If we only knew what was true
& would not hurt other people.
Is it not obvious I am not a mirror?

BYSTANDER

Standing by
To avoid being flattened
By the steamrollers of History,
You cannot win for love nor money.
Who can?

You wonder
As a not so innocent bystander:
How I am going to get whacked.
Of course, When the parade
Passes by

Hurrah! Hurrah!
If you were not on the sidelines,
Tossing your hat into the air,
Who will the people in power
Wave to?

ASK ALEXA

My 18 month old grandson
Runs into my living room,
Stops, turns,
Points to the round gray Echo.
He wants music.

I speak: Alexa, play
"The wheels of the bus
Go round & round"
&, like magic, the song
Starts playing. Mateo
Lowers his rump
& then pulls himself up,
Smiling, laughing,
I slap my knee,
He slaps my knee,
I tap the top of his head,
He taps the top of his head,
Lowers his rump,
Straightens up,
I slap my knee,
He slaps my knee,
I tap the top of his head,
He taps the top of his head,
My son enters the room,
 Surveys our vaudeville act,
Smiles, nods his head
Knowingly. The wheels
Of generations
Go round & round.

PHARMA

A filing cabinet jumped in front of my car.
Jesus! I thought. Just my luck
To run down everything from A to Z.

MY LIFE WITH THE BIG CATS

"Better were it to be eaten by tigers
Than to fall into our present condition."
—William Beckford's character in *Vathek*

Fame circus travels city
To city,
Time-smeared children

Applaud, whistle,
As the whip of reason.
Rips me.

Readers stomp, whoop
Demanding,
As my heart jumps

Thru hoops of fire,
More blood
Hero to nobody,

My scarred self
Limps
From one false hope
To another. My mistakes
Have sharpened
Their teeth on bars

Of Life's large cage.
Once
In a great while,

A tiger thought breaks
Free. *Grrrr.*
Roar. Howl. Claws

Scratch the surface
Of lost loves,
Friends becoming extinct.

Sorry.
I work mostly from anger,
& the world

Burns not so bright.
Take down
Tent poles, roll canvas,

Feed the animals,
Feed myself,
Count the tickets sold.

Another small town waits.

NIGHTWALKERS

Under this heavy stone of sky,
Women singing & dancing,
Chanting from the forest:

    Tata, mpembe,
    Tata, mpembe
    Kabillande!

My parents dead
For many decades now,
But I feel them beckoning.
I do not wish to go.

    Ngami waya mama.

Nightwalkers pound the earth,
The ground shakes.

Who has heard the Yoloche?
I do not know
What the women are chanting.
All I know is

There are many other worlds
To live in.

THE CHART

Geography does not lie.
Where is there a river
Without a name?

Still, there is a map,
The great star chart
Surrounded by constellations

That tells us not where we are
But who we are.
Somewhere between Perseus

With his shiny shield
Turning flesh to stone,
& 55 Cancri

Some 41 light years away.
No matter where we are
Always light falls,

Or we cd never see
Other lives casting shadows
Over everything

We are or shall become.
When it comes
To grief or to joy

One inch equals one mile.

THE INCREDIBLE SHRINKING POEM

1957: I must have been 14 or 15
When *The Incredible Shrinking Man,*
Starring Grant Williams,
Made it to my local movie house.
65 years later, I still see
The slaying of a giant tarantula
By a tiny man with a sewing needle.
Ironies of ironies:
Now I am the shrinking man,
Losing a fraction of my height
Year after year.
My cat licks its tongue.

HAUNTINGS

So much of my life
Is far out of reach,
But we all have our ghosts.
No doubt you have heard
Of Hamlet's father
At ungodly hours,
(If there are ungodly hours)
 Stalking the battlements.
But is it not true
We place heavy demands
Upon the shoulders
Of those we love?

I remember my own father
Spelling out as best he could
What he wanted me do
After he was dead.
A chilling evening.
He wanted to be certain
My younger sisters
Wd always have a home
To return to – if they had to return.

Knock, knock.
Who goes there?

My mother & her mother
Sat at night at our kitchen table,
Sharing a beer, talking
In hushed tones
In ways that frightened
My 10 year old self
Behind glass doors
That separated my bedroom
From the kitchen.
 O hear! O hear!
 It's over. It's over.

How many ghosts does it take
To haunt the human heart?

50 DEGREES OF SEPARATION

First snow of the season:
The logic of mortality
Hangs heavy on the air,
While all about me
Long stretches of earth
Stirring with subtle breathings,
Reminding us of seasons gone.

Reminding us roots of heaven
Do not reach down
As deep as we wish.
What does it matter who I am,
On the walls of galaxies
No Wanted Posters
Bearing my photo & fingerprints.

As I grow into one more decade
My life shapes & shifts
In garments so loose,
So lightweight
I can slip easily in & out,
Imagining seas so remote
That frightened sailors chant

"Below forty degrees latitude,
There is no law.
Below fifty degrees
There is no God."

AMBITION

This little verse
Has no ambitions
Whatsoever,

Resting in anthologies
Or in little magazines
Held together

By staples,
It merely
Wants to be

Whatever it is.

BAD ENDS

So many poems
Come to bad ends.
It is difficult to know
Where to begin.

FLY ASH

Divas are rehearsing
Mass extermination,
Fly ash & plutonium
From one end of the globe
To the other.

Even as I speak to you,
Esteemed leaders
Are rewriting history,
Drawing thick lines
Thru what really happened.

Mornings, once alive
With sunlight,
Darken over our heads,
Unnatural stillness
In the air.

Warning perhaps
Our happiness shd not depend

Upon the weather.
Finally a storm
Breaks over the lake

& far-away mountains.
Aldo Leopold says:
"Only the mountains
Have lived long enough
To listen objectively

To the howl of a wolf."
Years later. when I inquire
What the words mean,
The answer is: I am living
Among wolves.

CARPE DIEM

I am writing for today only,
If I cd only remember
What day it is.

A POEM NOT ABOUT A MONSOON

Monday: Sept. 2nd, 2003--
Heavy rain in Manhattan.
My wife, dressing for work,
Says: "It's a monsoon!"

It is not a monsoon.
Our sons have left
For college. It is
The empty house talking.

SAHARA

This morning – is it Thursday? –
I am crossing by foot
The Sahara of my imagination
Where one mirage
Follows another in rapid order –
Palm trees, dancing camels,
Women in dark veils
& see-thru trousers, my harem!
All, all a mirage
Except my desire not to die
In great pain.

CHANGE OF ADDRESS

I am moving into the middle of the ocean.
Since I have done so little
To improve human suffering,
I have decided to spend
The rest of my life as a lighthouse.

OUT OF TOUCH

Did Nehru visit Naurau?
She laughs
& talks about a man

We both know. She speaks
In such a way
I realize he was once

Her lover. Decades
Of revolving doors pass,
Persons enter our lives,

Then leave. What becomes
Of them?
Why did we fall out of touch?

We start families
& become insular.
Old friends move & addresses

Get lost, email is returned,
The harbor
Is overcrowded, ships

Unloading new cargoes
In out-of-the-way
Ports. An island

In the western Pacific,
Nauru
Is the world's smallest republic.

Persons too become islands.
In my small craft,
No matter how much I row

I can never reach them.

WIRELESS

On my plastic Philco radio,
The Shadow knew
What evil lurks in the hearts of men.

I am older now, the Philco gone,
But even I know
That evil does not always lurk;

Often it is right out in the open,
Behind barbed wire,
Or spoken openly to a crowd.

A madman, hammers his fist,
Denounces Jews
Or Blacks or Muslims. At night

In fields, men in white hoods
Burn a cross,
Uncoil rope for a lynching.

Before it was called radio,
We listened
To speech on a wireless;

Before it was called Evil,
It was called
The marriage of Fear to Hatred.

HOW TO RUIN A PERFECTLY FINE POEM

Oh for a merry whistling
With pipers out of tune.
So here I am, stout-hearted,
Trotting out tired adjectives
About the arrival of Spring
With its fur, fuzz &
Well-soiled Earth
Up to its ears with hurly-burly
Buzz & burr of new lives,
Crush of quarreling winds
Across the scheme of things
When all of sudden
Buffalo Bill, all aglitter
Rides in & out, back & forth,
Ruining a perfectly fine poem.

MUGGED

I do not know
Why I'm being held up.
I have so little
Going for me,
Am down to
My last few bucks.
Haven't sold a poem
In decades. Can't live
By swallowing staples
From little mags.
My Muse must have
Ratted on me.

But here I am
Staring down the barrel
Of an unabridged dictionary,
All those riches!
I have nothing to add.
"Your poetry or
Your life." I say:
"Go ahead, shoot;
I cannot think
Of a better way to die
Than to be gunned down
Somewhere between
Ochlocracy & Opera.

ABOUT THE AUTHOR

Louis Phillips, a widely published poet, playwright, and short story writer, has written some 50 books for children and adults. Among his published works are: six collections of short stories – *A Dream of Countries Where No One Dare Live* (SMU Press), *The Bus to the Moon* (Fort Schuyler Press), *The Woman Who Wrote King Lear and Other Stories* (Pleasure Boat Studio), *Must I Weep for The Dancing Bear* (Pleasure Boat Studio), *Galahad in the City of Tigers*, and *Sheathed Bayonets* (World Audience). *Hot Corner*, a collection of his baseball writings, and *R.I.P.* (a sequence of poems about Rip Van Winkle) from Livingston Press; *The Envoi Messages, The Ballroom in St. Patrick's Cathedral* and *The Last of The Marx Brothers' Writers*, full-length plays, (Broadway Play Publishers). *Fireworks in Some Particulars* (Fort Schuyler Press) is a collection of poetry, short stores, and humor pieces. That book also contains his play – *God Have Mercy on the June-Bug*. Pleasure Boat Studio has published *The Domain of Silence/The Domain of Absence: New & Selected Poems*, and *The Domain Of Small Mercies: New & Selected Poems*. Read more about Louis Phillips' numerous World Audience books on his Wikipedia page or his web site: www. louis-phillips.com.

BOOKS BY LOUIS PHILLIPS
PUBLISHED BY WORLD AUDIENCE PUBLISHERS

The Audience Book of Theater Quotations
American Elegies (poems)
The Death of the Siamese Twins & Other Plays
The Kilroy Sonata (poems)
Hollywood Scandals (plays)
The Moon Nobody Wanted
Honduras & Other Plays
Late Night in the Rain Forest (play)
The Collaborators (play)
The Secret Voyage of Melvin Moonmist
The Last Lion
Robot 9 in Wonderland
How Wide the Meadow (poems)
Caesar, Caesar, Caesar (play)
Narragansett 1937 (play)
Dr. Jazz: A Comedy (play)
Canary in the Mine: A Collection of Humor
Galahad in the City of Tigers (short stories)
Quick Flicks (clerihews)
The Pleasure of His Company (the off-beat Shakespeare book)
Dial M for Mysteries
The Oarsmen & Other Plays
Icebergs and Other Plays
Rowing to the Silly Islands (light verse)
It Takes a Lot of Paper to Gift Wrap an Elephant (children's book)
Sheathed Bayonets & Other Stories

4 (stories, plays, poems)
Procession (a film script)
Sentenced (Reading, Writing, and Book Publishing)
La Triviata: The Book of Off-Beat Fun Quizzes—(first edition, second edition)
The Book of Epigraphs
Music of Light Regret (poems)

Made in the USA
Middletown, DE
26 August 2024